SOON, YOUR HANDS

by **Jonathan Stutzman**

illustrated by **Elizabeth Lilly**

Alfred A. Knopf
New York

Tonight

I hold your hands,
so small
they fit inside my own.

But soon,

your hands will grow.
And learn.

Soon, your hands will make mistakes

and messes

and, also, masterpieces.

Some tiny.

Some average.

Some bold and big

and wondrous.

And they will grow.

Soon, your hands will discover the world

and the shapes of living things.

Your hands will feel the warmth of the earth,

the chill of the moving sky.

The roaring thunder

of the deep, deep ocean.

Soon, your hands will make music.

They will throw colors like magic.

They will tell stories only you know how to tell.

And they will grow.

Soon, your hands will pull you up closer to the stars,

so that you will know endings.

Soon.

They will dig down into the dirt
so that you will know beginnings.

Soon, your hands will learn the importance of a heartbeat,

of kindness and love.

They will learn how to
break bread,

give water,

and warm the tiniest of trembles.

They will help and heal

and hold life gently.

And they will grow.

Soon.

Soon, my hands will let go of yours,
and you will do all these things

and more.

REYNA

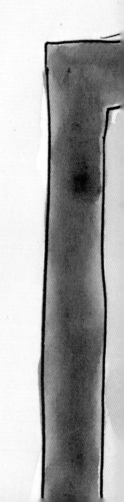

TY

ERIC

But tonight,

tonight I hold your hands, so small

they fit inside my own.

To Elizabeth Lilly: Keep using your hands to create
beautiful things, and throwing colors like magic.
—J.S.

To Steph, for holding my hand during
the making of this book.
Love,
Lizard Beth
—E.L.

THIS IS A BORZOI BOOK PUBLISHED BY ALFRED A. KNOPF

Text copyright © 2023 by Jonathan Stutzman

Jacket art and interior illustrations copyright © 2023 by Elizabeth Lilly

All rights reserved. Published in the United States by Alfred A. Knopf, an imprint of Random House Children's Books,
a division of Penguin Random House LLC, New York.

Knopf, Borzoi Books, and the colophon are registered trademarks of Penguin Random House LLC.

Visit us on the Web! rhcbooks.com

Educators and librarians, for a variety of teaching tools, visit us at RHTeachersLibrarians.com

Library of Congress Cataloging-in-Publication Data is available upon request.
ISBN 978-0-593-42707-1 (trade)—ISBN 978-0-593-42708-8 (lib. bdg.)—ISBN 978-0-593-42709-5 (ebook)

The text of this book is set in 17-point Recoleta.
These illustrations were created using a nib pen, black Daler-Rowney ink, and Grumbacher watercolors.
Book design by Elizabeth Tardiff

MANUFACTURED IN CHINA
10 9 8 7 6 5 4 3 2 1

First Edition

American Sign Language Glossary

Reyna is deaf and speaks American Sign Language (ASL) with her family. Different combinations of arm and hand movements indicate different words.

Here are some words Reyna and her parents say in the book and how to sign them:

Mami says "cat."

1. Put your hand near your nose, palm facing outward.
2. Pinch your thumb and index finger together, leaving your other three fingers up.
3. Move your hand outward from your face.

Mami says "Take off your hearing aid."

1. Close your hand in a fist.
2. Put up your index finger.
3. Bend down the tip of your index finger in a hook shape.
4. Hook your index finger behind your ear in the shape of a hearing aid.
5. Move your arm away from your body.

Papi says "Let's go."

1. Open your hand in front of your face, palm facing inward.
2. Tilt your hand so your thumb is near your nose and your four fingers are near your forehead.
3. Pinch your four fingers and your thumb together while moving your hand away from your body and toward the place that you're going.